W9-BRV-367

Mermaid KINGDOM

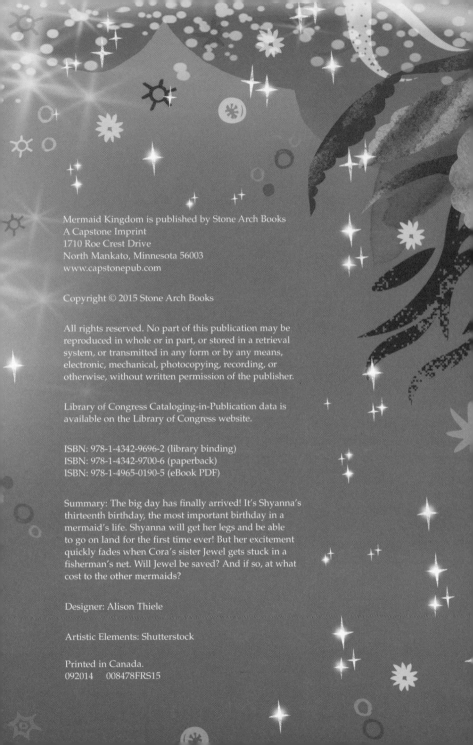

Mermaid Kingdom is published by Stone Arch Books
A Capstone Imprint
1710 Roe Crest Drive
North Mankato, Minnesota 56003
www.capstonepub.com

Copyright © 2015 Stone Arch Books

All rights reserved. No part of this publication may be
reproduced in whole or in part, or stored in a retrieval
system, or transmitted in any form or by any means,
electronic, mechanical, photocopying, recording, or
otherwise, without written permission of the publisher.

Library of Congress Cataloging-in-Publication data is
available on the Library of Congress website.

ISBN: 978-1-4342-9696-2 (library binding)
ISBN: 978-1-4342-9700-6 (paperback)
ISBN: 978-1-4965-0190-5 (eBook PDF)

Summary: The big day has finally arrived! It's Shyanna's
thirteenth birthday, the most important birthday in a
mermaid's life. Shyanna will get her legs and be able
to go on land for the first time ever! But her excitement
quickly fades when Cora's sister Jewel gets stuck in a
fisherman's net. Will Jewel be saved? And if so, at what
cost to the other mermaids?

Designer: Alison Thiele

Artistic Elements: Shutterstock

Printed in Canada.
092014   008478FRS15

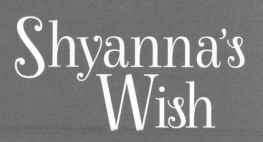

Shyanna's Wish

by Janet Gurtler

illustrated by Katie Wood

3 1150 01446 3380

STONE ARCH BOOKS
a capstone imprint

BOISE PUBLIC LIBRARY

Mermaid Life

⭐ Mermaid Kingdom refers to all the kingdoms in the sea, including Neptunia, Caspian, Hercules, Titania, and Nessland. Each kingdom has a king and queen who live in a castle. Merpeople live in caves.

⭐ Mermaids get their legs on their thirteenth birthdays at the stroke of midnight. It's a celebration when the mermaid makes her first voyage onto land. After their thirteenth birthdays, mermaids can go on land for short periods of time but must be very careful.

⭐ If a mermaid goes on land before her thirteenth birthday, she will get her legs early and never get her tail back. She will lose all memories of being a mermaid and will be human forever.

BOISE PUBLIC LIBRARY

⭐ Mermaids are able to stay on land with legs for no more than forty-eight hours. Any longer and they will not be able to get their tails back and will be human forever. They will lose all memories of being a mermaid.

⭐ If they fall in love, merpeople and humans can marry and have babies (with special permission from the king and queen of their kingdom). Their babies are half-human and half-merperson. However, this love must be the strongest love possible in order for it to be approved by the king and queen.

⭐ Half-human mermaids are able to go on land indefinitely and can change back to a mermaid anytime. However, they are not allowed to tell other humans about the mermaid world unless they have special permission from the king and queen.

Chapter One

It was almost the big day! Only one more night
until my birthday! Everyone loves to have a birthday,
but this year was extra special because I was going to
turn thirteen. In Mermaid Kingdom, turning thirteen
is a VBD (very big deal). At midnight on thirteenth
birthdays, merpeople go to land and get to use legs
for the first time. After that, our legs can be used
on land for a few hours at a time. I was so excited to
be able to join my best friends, Rachel and Cora, for
adventures on land.

I loved being a mermaid and I loved the ocean, but there was something about breathing air and having legs that intrigued me, too.

"Shyanna!" my mom called while I braided my hair and imagined myself skipping on the beach.

"What's up, Mom?" I shouted from my room as I finished up my hair. I imagined she was curious about which song I'd selected to sing at my midnight leg ceremony. The leg ceremony was totally magical.

"Have you finished with the shell decorations you and the girls were working on for the Neptunia Day parade?" my mom called.

I rolled my eyes at the reflection in my mirror. The mirror was a treasure my dad had found in an old shipwreck. He'd given it to me right before he disappeared two years earlier.

Neptunia may have been the best kingdom in the ocean, but there were always dangers underwater. From humans and nets to sharks and storms, the ocean was a dangerous place to live. Anything could happen at any time, and nobody really knows what happened to my dad. Although it's getting easier, my mom and I still miss him every day.

"They're done," I called. "We left them on the kitchen table."

"Thank goodness. We have to finish up all the details for the Queen's float this morning. You girls are lifesavers!" she called. "I was up so late last night going over all the last minute details with the parade committee. I never could have done them on my own." She swam into my room and smiled at me. "You look so beautiful." She swam closer and kissed me on the cheek. "I can't believe it's your last day as a twelve-year-old mergirl!"

Mom was always super busy for Neptunia Day because she was the leader of the parade committee. Unfortunately, this year Neptunia Day fell on the same day as my birthday. It was kind of overshadowing my big day, but I was trying hard not to let it ruin things.

We looked at each other in my mirror, and then she sighed. "I wish I didn't have to be so busy with the parade committee today. But I have to finish up all the float preparations. The Queen likes things to be perfect. Speaking of perfect, we'll make all the final arrangements for your leg ceremony tonight. Okay? You must be so excited!"

"I really am, " I said. "I can't wait to have legs so I can go with Rachel and Cora to see Owen on land and meet his friends!"

Owen was Rachel's best friend and a human. Because Rachel was half-human and half-mermaid, she could go on land whenever she wanted for as long as she wanted. That's how she met Owen. Rachel often felt weird because she was both human and mermaid, but I thought it was amazing and was a little jealous of her.

"Well, you won't see Owen and any of his friends at your leg ceremony," she said. "It's too late at night, and Owen and his friends will be sleeping."

"I know that," I told her. "I meant later. When I go to land with Cora and Rachel. Also, I decided on a small leg ceremony. Just Rachel and Cora and their families."

"Sounds good," she said, but I could tell she was losing focus.

"I'm so excited you're going on land with me. I know it's been a long time for you," I continued, hoping to spend a little more time with my mom before she had to leave again.

"Mm hmm. Good." She nodded as she checked through the shell purse slung over her shoulder. "So what are you doing today?"

"I'm meeting Cora and Rachel at Walrus Waterpark to hang out and go over my plans. We might go swim with dolphins later or take Cora's sisters to watch sea turtles."

"Oh darn," my mom said, clearly not even listening. "I forgot the list with the order of the parade floats." She swam closer and kissed my

forehead again. "I have to find it before I go. Sorry I'm so wrapped up in Neptunia Day," she added.

"It's okay," I said, even though I wished my birthday didn't coincide with Neptunia Day. It was a great day of celebration for our castle, with a big parade and lots of other fun events. It went on all day and late into the night. And I didn't want to seem selfish, but it seemed like with the preparations and timing, everyone was forgetting about my birthday. Thirteen was a huge deal, and getting my legs for the first time was an even bigger deal.

"I have to run," Mom said. "I'm so sorry, but we'll talk about everything you've planned at our spa appointment tomorrow. Meanwhile, I'm so glad Rachel and Cora are around to help you with your plans. You're so lucky to have them. Such great best friends." She wiped away a smear of algae on my mirror and frowned. "It's been such a long time since I've been on land." Her lips turned down more, and she sighed.

"I'll see you later. Have a good day," she said absently as she swam off to fetch the decorations.

My mom seemed even more distracted than usual, which didn't make me feel confident that my birthday plans would work out. The leg ceremony was such a big deal, and without my mom I couldn't do it. Her distraction made me feel nervous — very, very nervous.

Chapter Two

"Hey, almost-birthday girl!" Cora said when I swam into Walrus Waterpark. As always, Cora's baby sister was tucked under her arm and another sister swam in front of her, giggling as she tried to get away.

"I can't believe my mom volunteered to work with yours on the parade committee this year," Cora said. "Now I'm stuck looking after my sisters all day long." She sighed dramatically as she put Jewel into the baby swing and then pushed her other two sisters.

For once I agreed with her. I loved Cora's sisters despite all their shenanigans, but they were a lot of work. I always wished I had sisters of my own, but today I kind of wanted things to be about my plans.

"Can you take them with us to swim with the dolphins later?" I asked, kind of knowing the answer already. I swam over and took over Jewel's swing.

"No. They're too young. We'll have to do it another time," Cora said.

I nodded, trying not to show my disappointment. "I wonder where Rachel is," I said, looking around the park. "She's not usually late."

"She's been working on a new number for the Spirit Squad," Cora said. "She probably lost track of time."

Rachel was kind of obsessed with coming up with new routines for the group to perform. We were all on the squad, but Rachel was the most involved.

"Oh," I said, trying not to show the resentment that was creeping around my insides. I was bummed that no one seemed to be very concerned about my birthday or seemed to want to help with my plans. I'd been looking forward to it for as long as I could remember. Turning thirteen and having your leg ceremony was so important, and nobody seemed to care. Not my mom, and not my best friends.

"What are you wearing to the parade?" Cora asked as she pushed one sister in the swing and swam over quickly to push the others beside her.

I sighed, sick of Neptunia Day and all its birthday attention robbing. I wanted to talk about what I should wear to my leg ceremony, not the stupid parade. I wanted to talk about how I should do my hair and what color I should paint my nails. I was so over the parade, and it hadn't even started yet.

"I don't know," I told Cora, rolling my eyes just a little. "My mom and I are going to the spa before the parade, and I hadn't really thought about it too much. I'm more concerned about what I'm going to wear that night."

I was just about to tell Cora what happened with my mom and how I was feeling about my leg ceremony when Rachel swam into the park.

"Sorry I'm late!" she cried before I could mutter any more complaints about my birthday plans. Rachel swam to the swings and did a flip in front of the sisters to make them laugh. Her long red hair flowed out behind her. I wished I could get my hair to curl and spring freely like hers. It would be the perfect style for my leg ceremony.

"I was at Cassie's cave," Rachel said. Cassie was the songwriter for the Spirit Squad, and she and Rachel spent lots of time working together.

I was happy Rachel was making new friends. She'd had a hard time with some of the merkids when she and her dad moved to Neptunia. Most of us thought it was cool she was half-human and could use her legs on land whenever she wanted to. But some merkids hadn't been so nice about it, and Rachel had some trust issues.

I was glad Rachel loved the Spirit Squad and had made new friends, but was it wrong that I kind of wanted some of her attention on me now?

Rachel and Cora both played with me for a while, but they were both really distracted. Before long they both left, and my birthday had hardly even been mentioned.

Chapter Three

That night Mom got home late again. She was exhausted from all her hard work with the parade committee. We ate leftovers and decided to talk about my birthday plans in the morning because she was too tired. So much for getting everything in order for my birthday. I felt like nobody had time for me, and it was really starting to make me sad.

Mom wanted to go to bed early, so I pretended I was tired too and ended up sadly staring at the ceiling until late in the night.

When I opened my eyes in the morning, I stretched my arms and smiled. It was my birthday! I was thirteen! I would finally get my legs!

I swam out of bed. "Mom?" I called.

No one answered. The cave was quiet.

I swam from my room. I swam into the kitchen. There was a note on the table next to a bowl and my favorite kind of cereal.

"Happy Birthday, Shyanna! I had to go check out a problem with the Queen's float. I'll be back as soon as I can. Be ready to go to the spa when I get home!"

Things were too silent and unfestive. This was not how I wanted my birthday to start. I tried not to be disappointed and softly hummed the "Happy Birthday" song to myself as I ate. I tried to enjoy the peace and quiet.

After breakfast, I swam to the front yard. It was even quiet out there. The only things I saw were

some small snails playing a slow and noiseless game of hide-and-seek. I guessed that everyone was too busy getting things in order for Neptunia Day to care about my birthday.

I felt eyes on me and looked around hopefully, but it was only a scallop watching me. He was bright and beautiful with his fan-shaped shell, so I waved hello. I hoped he'd come over and offer some company, but he ignored my gesture and swam away, opening and closing his shell to move. I have never felt so lonely in my life!

I sighed, but then I heard the phone ringing from inside our cave. It had to be Rachel or Cora, and they'd probably burst into the birthday song as soon as I picked it up. I hurried inside and grabbed the phone with a big smile on my face.

"Hello?" I sang.

"Shyanna?" It was my mom. And I could tell she wasn't happy just by the way she said my name.

"Hi, Mom," I said. "Are you okay?

"I'm fine, Shy. Things have just gotten crazy around here. We have a bit of an emergency. A hammerhead shark smashed up the Queen's float. We're working really hard to get it fixed, but I don't know how long I'm going to be delayed. I'm trying to get away, but there's no one else to handle things. Do you think . . . would you mind terribly if one of the girls went to the spa in my place? I feel so badly, but I have no idea how long I'll take, and I don't want you to miss your appointment because of me."

My heart sank to the ocean floor. "Of course not, Mom. Don't worry about it. I'll ask Rachel or Cora to come. It'll be fine. Fun!"

I didn't mention that we were supposed to finalize my plans for the leg ceremony. I still had to choose my song, and we hadn't figured out what Mom was going to wear to coordinate with my outfit for our walk on land together.

"Cora's mom is with me," Mom went on, "so Cora's probably busy watching her sisters. I'm sure

Rachel will love it, though! Have fun. I'll be home as soon as I can!" Then she hung up the phone.

A tear slid out of my eye as I put the phone down. She hadn't even said goodbye.

I called Rachel, but her dad answered. "Sorry, Shyanna," he said. "Rachel went to land to see Owen. He has some new songs to teach her, and she wanted to incorporate them into the new Spirit Squad routine. She sure loves that group. But hey, happy birthday! Today's the big day! Can't wait to see you on your new legs tonight!"

"Thanks, Mr. Marlin," I said, thankful that at least someone was around to wish me a happy birthday. I seriously considered asking him to go to the spa with me, but decided that would be way too awkward for both of us.

I sighed when I hung up the phone, feeling like the biggest loser in Mermaid Kingdom. It was my birthday, and I was all alone! My birthday was a complete disaster.

I knew I could ask another mergirl to go with me to the spa. I had plenty of friends from school, and anyone would be happy to have a free spa date. But it didn't feel right to ask just anyone. And besides, no one else had been invited to my leg ceremony. It seemed selfish and last minute to ask someone else to join me to celebrate now.

I'd go alone. How bad could it be?

Chapter Four

"You'll start your song quietly as you emerge from the water at exactly midnight," Star Fishery, the beautician at the spa explained as she painted my fingernails.

Star had been thrilled when she found out it was my birthday. She actually shouted loudly with joy when I told her I was thirteen. When she heard about my mom's emergency, she immediately started helping me plan my leg ceremony. She even helped me decide on my song and insisted I practice singing.

Despite my stage fright and all the other mermaids in the spa, I managed to sing the whole thing out loud. Everyone clapped when I was done and assured me I would have the most perfect leg ceremony ever.

"When you get your legs, you start to build up the song at a louder crescendo. The moon is full tonight, so you'll be lit by soft glowing light," Star said. "We'll undo your braids so your hair will flow all curly and bouncy around your pretty face." She giggled with delight, and her enthusiasm was infectious and warmed my woeful heart. "It will be magical — completely magical and unforgettable. The way every leg ceremony is meant to be."

"Do you really think so?" I asked, starting to feel a lot better about my special day. Leave it to Star to bring the magic back.

"I do," she said. "I know you wish your mama was here, but I'm going to help you and make you so beautiful it will be a night you'll never forget.

What color is your outfit? I'll apply matching starfish decals on your nails!"

I told her what I planned to wear: the purple shell top and matching necklaces. She nodded with enthusiasm. She rubbed my tail with sparkly oil and added rainbow glitter to my hair. She said the hair glitter would last all day and shimmer in the light of the full moon. The excitement in the spa helped me get in the mood for the day, and my sadness about being forgotten disappeared.

As I got up from the chair, everyone cheered and whistled. Then Star started off a round of "Happy Birthday" and everyone sang. I floated out of the shop and swam back toward my cave, finally feeling special and happy.

With all the extra work Star put in at the spa, I was home a little later than expected. I swam in the front door of the cave, excited to show my mom how incredible I looked.

"Mom!" I sang when I swam into our cave,

already holding out my hand so she could admire my birthday nails up close. I wasn't going to dwell on the fact that it was the mermaid at the spa who helped me plan the final details for my leg ceremony. Nothing could take away from my big day now! Everything was set and it was going to be perfect.

"Mom?" I shouted again.

There was no answer. In fact, our cave was eerily quiet.

I swam into the kitchen. "Mom?" I said, but no one said a word. I swam around the cave and realized, with heart-crushing certainty, that she wasn't home.

There was no clam cake. There were no sea balloons or presents on the table. The Neptunia Day parade was more important to her than I was. All of my excitement from the spa evaporated in one big sigh.

I didn't want to cry, but I could barely hold back the tears anymore.

I grabbed the phone and called Rachel's cave. Maybe her dad knew where my mom was. No one at the Marlin residence answered. I frowned and then dialed Cora's number. No one picked up there, either. Were they all out enjoying the Neptunia Day festivities without me? Had they completely forgotten about my birthday? I glanced at the clock as I put the phone back on the table.

It was already past dinnertime, and I hadn't heard from my two best friends or my mom in hours. I swam slowly to my room, catching a reflection of my shimmering tail in my special mirror on the cave wall.

If my dad was here, would I be all alone on my thirteenth birthday? I swam inside my room, my heart heavy and tears bubbling up in the corners of my eyes.

"Shyanna!" a voice shouted from outside the cave.

I frowned. Was that Rachel's voice? It sounded panicked.

I swam toward my door as Rachel burst inside.

"Rachel!" I cried. Finally, someone had come to see me on my birthday! But then I saw her face. It was pale and worried. She didn't look happy or excited. She looked terrified. What was going on?

"Thank goodness you're here!" she said.

I frowned, but before I could ask what was wrong, she grabbed my hand and pulled me.

"Come on. We have to go. Fast! Jewel is trapped in a fishing net!" she shouted. "We're too big to get her out. We need you. You're her last hope."

Chapter Five

My heart pounded like waves crashing onto shore as Rachel and I swam up through the water to the fishing net where Jewel was stuck.

"Cora and I tried to get her out, but we're too big," Rachel explained as we swam faster than I thought I could swim. "You are the only one small enough to help her. Your mom is there, and my dad and Cora's family, but no one can get to her."

"What was everyone doing when she got stuck?" I asked.

She glanced at me. "I'll explain later."

We swam so quickly that everything was a blur, and in a few minutes we reached the net. My tail ached, and the shine and shimmer from the spa had completely disappeared from kicking so hard, but none of that mattered when I saw Jewel.

Baby Jewel was inside a net, trapped and squished up against hundreds of fish of various sizes. Her whole family and my mom and Rachel's dad were gathered outside of the net, following it with terrified helpless looks on their faces as it dragged along the ocean floor. It was eerily quiet as the net moved, like it was all a bad dream. All the nearby sea creatures were hiding, frightened.

Cora was at my side in an instant when she saw me. "Oh, Shyanna!" she cried. "We've tried and tried, but we're too big to slip into the net. Jewel can't make her way out alone. She doesn't understand how, and she's too worked up to listen to us. She needs someone to go in and get her."

"I'll go," I said without hesitation. Being small for my age was finally a benefit for once. On top of being small, I was really flexible. It was my time to step up and help.

"Be careful, Shyanna," my mom said, patting my shoulder as I swam by.

Cora's mom had three little mergirls clinging to her, and Cora's dad had his arm around her. "Please help," he whispered. I nodded and swam past. There was no time to talk. Rachel and Cora swam with me to the net.

"If you can slip inside the hole, you can help get Jewel out," Cora said. Her voice was strained and nervous. "You have to get her out!"

I nodded and swam to the net, grabbing at the thick scratchy rope. It pulled away from my hands as if it sensed what I was about to do, almost taking my fingernails right off.

"Oh!" I shouted, surprised. When I pulled my hand back, I caught a glimpse of my nails. My new manicure was destroyed, but I knew that didn't matter. The only thing that mattered right now was Jewel.

"The boat is trolling, so it sometimes makes sudden moves like that," Cora told me. "It's okay. Try again. Hurry."

I nodded and swam to the rope. It was rough and wiry and totally inflexible. No wonder the girls couldn't sneak through. I glanced around at the holes to see if some were bigger than others. There was one that seemed a bit larger. It was going to be a tight fit, but I knew I could do it.

I squeezed my head in without too much of a problem and then wiggled around and got my body through. The rope scratched and burned my tail, but I ignored the pain and reached down. My fins were cut up and sore, but I remembered a trick from when I used to play hide-and-seek. I took a deep breath and folded my tail in half.

I was in!

"Jewel!" I cried and started shoving fish out of my way.

Jewel was crying. Her tail was tangled in the rope, and she couldn't swim away from it. Fish were pressed against each other, all of them struggling to get out and causing a bigger tangle.

I gritted my teeth and pressed through the fish to get to Jewel. I wrapped my arms around her and tugged, but she shrieked loudly when I pulled her. I had to get closer to get her tail loose.

Outside the net I heard the girls yelling, and our mothers' cries got louder and louder. I didn't pay attention. I had to focus on Jewel. As gently as I could, I unsnagged Jewel and then held her in my arms.

"Hey, little girl," I said and smiled to try to calm her down.

"Shyanna!" Cora called.

I looked through layers of fish at the holes in the thick rope as I held Jewel close. "You're moving,"

Cora cried, pointing up. "The net is being pulled to the surface. You need to hurry!"

I realized Cora was swimming higher as she yelled, her tail wiggling fast to keep up with the net as it was being pulled closer to the surface. Rachel was a few feet below her, swimming hard to try to catch up.

"Get out!" Cora shouted. "You have to get out before you reach the surface or the humans will see you!"

I squeezed through tons of little fish and dove toward the bottom of the net, holding Jewel tightly the entire time.

"The net is almost out of the water!" Cora cried. "No!"

Chapter Six

I put my head down and swam faster, protecting

Jewel with my arms. I managed to squeeze through

a wall of fish, and my head popped through a hole. I

was going to make it! I pushed halfway through and

was about to fold my fin to finish my escape from the

net when Jewel screamed. Her torn tail was snagged

on the wiry rope again.

I gently tugged her, trying to pull her through,

but she cried louder. I glanced up in a panic. The

rope was almost out of the water. I could see the

reflection of the sun from below the water. We were close to the surface, and I was starting to panic.

I struggled to free Jewel without hurting her as we continued to move up. I held my breath. There was no way I was going to let her go on her own. Merpeople were yelling beneath us, but I didn't stop trying. I finally managed to pull her tail free, but a split second later realized that it was too late. The top of my head was already out of the water.

Around me, the fish gasped. They couldn't breathe out of the water, because they were unable to adapt to oxygen from air the way merpeople could. I closed my eyes and waited to be exposed. We were going to be pulled out of the water, and there was nothing I could do about it. It wouldn't be long before the fishermen realized they'd caught more than a net full of fish.

Humans still thought merpeople were just legends. Once the humans spotted us, we would be risking the underwater world and putting all

merpeople in jeopardy. The Kings and Queens of Mermaid Kingdom couldn't allow that to happen, which was why they had created a magic spell. If we were exposed to humans and were caught, we would lose our tails and memories of being mermaids. We would be human forever, never able to return to the ocean. It would seem as if the fishermen had caught a young human girl and a baby. If we were spotted but escaped, we would never be able to get legs. We would never be able to leave the ocean.

Everything was happening so quickly. I closed my eyes as I waited to be pulled to the surface. It was my thirteenth birthday. The day that was supposed to be the happiest day of my life. Instead, I was trapped in a net, about to be exposed to humans and lose my memories — and all of my family and friends.

With renewed energy and panic, I opened my eyes, dipped my head underwater, pulled on Jewel, and managed to force our way to the bottom of the net and out of a small hole.

Suddenly there were loud noises from the boat above us. Something was causing a huge commotion. There was shouting and waves, and then a beautiful sound that was a little muffled under the water. As quickly as it had begun, the commotion stopped.

The net dropped and went down fast. The top of the net opened as we sailed downward. I held tightly to Jewel and swam out, following a big, excited school of fish to safety. It was a miracle!

"We're free!" I shouted when we were outside the net. "We're safe, Jewel!"

I did a couple of victory flips, and Jewel stopped crying. She started to giggle. Then I swam over to Cora, who was watching us with wide eyes. I held out Jewel. Cora took her baby sister from me and hugged her close.

When she looked up at me, there were tears dropping down her cheeks. She blinked quickly as she stared at me and then looked up toward the surface of the water.

"I'm so sorry, Shy," she said.

"What's wrong?" I frowned and glanced at Rachel to see what was going on, but she was crying, too.

"Your mom . . ." Cora said.

That was the sound I'd heard.

A sound I hadn't heard in a very, very long time, since before my dad disappeared.

It was my mom, singing.

Chapter Seven

"What happened?" I demanded, feeling even more panicked than I had felt trapped in the net with Jewel.

Cora was holding Jewel close. "Your mom was very brave. She saved you. She saved you and Jewel." Cora's family and Rachel's dad were swimming closer to us, yelling my name and Jewel's. But all I could think about was my mom.

I glanced down at the ocean below from where they approached. Large strands of coral reef

stretched up as if waving, and bright blue-cheeked butterflyfish swarmed around them, the scene colorful and deceptively beautiful. Up swam Cora's parents, their eyes on Jewel, looking relieved and exhausted. But when they glanced at me, I saw the tears and sadness in their eyes. Cora's mom grabbed Jewel from Cora's arms, crying and holding her tightly.

"Oh, Shyanna, thank you," she whispered.

"Where's my mom?" I yelled at everyone and no one at the same time, with a bad feeling in my fins. I knew. I knew where she was, but nobody would say it.

"She said she was going to cause a distraction," Rachel's dad said quietly.

Cora's dad swam close to me and patted my arm. "Oh, Shyanna, you saved Jewel. You saved our baby."

"Where's my mom?" I shouted again, my dread growing as I looked around at all the beautiful sea life surrounding me.

"She said she was going to shock the fishermen so they'd drop the net," Rachel's dad said. "We couldn't stop her. She swam out of the water, and she started to sing."

"It was her," I whispered.

"It was the most powerful thing I've ever heard," Rachel's dad said, his eyes sad but also filled with wonder. "I've never heard anything so beautiful in my life, and we were below the water. The humans above the water were so mesmerized by her singing that they dropped the net."

"But she didn't need to do that," I said. "I got free and saved Jewel."

"What a voice," Rachel's dad repeated, and everyone nodded solemnly.

I swallowed. "So my mom was seen by the humans? Singing?"

"She was," Rachel's dad said.

"And she's still up there?" I asked, barely able to get the words out.

"No." We all turned to see Rachel. She was breathing heavily. "I swam up. She wasn't in the boat. They saw her, but she stayed on a rock and escaped before they broke out of their spell."

"Thank goodness!" I sighed with relief. I had been thinking the absolute worst. I knew she would never be able to use her legs again, but at least she was alive!

"She's trapped in the ocean now, forever," Rachel said sadly.

"Where is she?" I asked.

"The King and Queen are with her. They left the Neptunia Day celebrations and came right away," Rachel said.

"Already?" I asked. It seemed like it had all happened so quickly. It *had* all happened so quickly.

Rachel nodded. "The magic used is serious. They were here seconds later. They had to make sure Neptunia was safe."

"But she saved me. She saved Jewel," I whispered.

"I know," Rachel said. "But it's a big offense, Shy. Exposing herself to humans. She got away, but the King and Queen don't know if the humans realized what she was. They don't think anyone will believe the fishermen if they talk about what they saw. But rules are rules. She was seen. She'll never be able to use her legs on land again."

Chapter Eight

I swam up closer to the surface. The sunset was rippling over the water above, creating a gorgeous array of colors. There was no wind and no waves. It was totally still and quiet. The boat was gone. There was no sign of the King and Queen or my mom. It was eerie.

"They must have gone back to the palace," Rachel said.

"I have to get to her," I cried. "I have to see my mom!"

My shredded tail hurt from scraping the rope and folding up to escape, but I moved through the water faster than a shark on a hunt. I truly had never moved so fast in my life. Rachel and Cora were right behind me, swimming just as fast.

We swam through the gates of Neptunia, and immediately the festive sounds of Neptunia Day filled my ears.

The parade was over and night had fallen, but the celebrations would last until the last merpeople went to their caves. There was music and cheering coming from games and rides all over the castle, everything from sea horse racing to seaweed braiding to coral reef Ferris wheels. It was absolutely magical. I wish I could stop and enjoy it, but there wasn't time.

I swam straight to the castle, but the guard at the front raised his hand when I got near. "The King and Queen have asked you to stay away while they deal with your mother's transgression," he said in a deep, solemn voice.

"Come with us," Cora's mom said. I turned to see that Cora's whole family and Rachel and her dad were right behind me. Cora's mom was still clinging tightly to Jewel.

"We will all be at the Bell residence," she said to the guard. "Please have the King and Queen inform Shyanna's mother that we are gathered there, waiting for her. She's a hero."

We swam through the castle, swimming past merpeople old and young who were smiling and enjoying Neptunia Day festivities. No one seemed to notice the look on my face. They all smiled and waved.

Thankfully they had no idea what had happened. They had no idea that the entire Mermaid Kingdom was nearly exposed to the human world. If anyone found out, it would be complete chaos.

We swam inside Cora's family cave, and her mom disappeared to put the babies to bed while her dad made us some hot cocoa.

After I had the last sip of my cocoa, my mom came swimming into the living room. I swam up to meet her. She held out her arms, and I slipped inside.

"Oh, Mom," I said, sobbing. She'd saved me and Jewel from being exposed, and for that I was grateful. But I felt guilty. If only I could have saved Jewel faster none of this would have happened.

Mom patted my tangled hair, her arms tightly around me. "It's okay, honey," she whispered. "It's okay." I felt a little like a merbaby instead of a teenage mermaid.

"But you'll never walk on land again," I said. Tears ran down my cheeks like a waterfall.

"Oh, Shyanna," Mom said. "I haven't been on land for a long time anyhow."

"But you could go if you wanted to until now," I said. "And that's a big difference."

"It doesn't matter, Shy," she said. "It really doesn't matter much to me. I was so worried about you and baby Jewel being caught, and I couldn't lose you.

I won't. Not you, too." She squeezed me tighter, and I knew we were both thinking about my dad.

I pulled back from her and looked into her eyes. "Your voice," I said. "Even from below, it was the most amazing sound. Rachel's dad said it was the most wonderful voice he's ever heard. And that's from a singing coach."

"That's an exaggeration," she said, blushing and looking shyly at the group.

"I don't think so," I told her. "Those humans were mesmerized. They didn't know what was happening. That's why they dropped the net." I hugged her tightly again and then pulled out of her arms. "Thank you, Mom. Thank you for saving us."

Cora's mom was crying. She swam over and embraced both of us. "It's my fault. I should have gone," Cora's mom said. "You saved my baby's life. And I did nothing."

My mom shook her head. "No. You were protecting the rest of your family. I was the closest to the surface.

And my husband always used to tell me my voice could save us from humans if we were ever spotted. I've always been too shy, but he used to love going off on treasure hunts and singing. Oh, how he'd sing. He would sing day and night."

She stared off into space for a moment, remembering him. "It had to be me," she whispered.

Cora's dad swam over and circled all of us in his arms. We were all shedding salty tears, both happy and sad at the same time.

"Holy catfish!" Cora yelled, startling all of us out of our group hug.

We all stared at Cora. "Do you realize what time it is?" she cried again, pointing at the shell clock on the wall. "There's less than an hour until midnight!" she screamed. "And it's Shyanna's thirteenth birthday. We have to get her to shore!"

Everyone started talking at once.

"Oh my goodness, I didn't even get to make her shrimp cake!" my mom yelled.

"And her presents are still at home," Rachel called back.

"Never mind all that! It can wait. Her leg ceremony can't!" Cora pointed out. Thank goodness for Cora. She was always the sensible one.

My mom started to cry again. "I never even helped you pick out your song or outfit, and I missed our spa date." She hid her face in her hands. "I'm so sorry, Shyanna. I was so busy with the parade problems, and then all of this. And now I can't even take you on land."

"You saved my life, Mom," I said. "I forgive you."

"She's right. You saved my sister and your daughter, so we'll feel bad about her birthday party later," Cora said. "Right now, we need to focus on getting her to land."

"Maybe we should clean her up at a bit first," Rachel said nicely.

They all looked at me, and I looked down at myself. I was a mess. My manicure was in shreds, my hair was crazy, and my once-shimmering tail was tattered and torn up.

"No," I said quietly. "There isn't time."

"You're right," Rachel said. "It doesn't matter what you look like. I mean, you're beautiful, just a little . . . um . . . messy. All that matters is that you're there. On land. At midnight."

"No," I repeated, a little louder.

My mom put an arm around me. "The girls can go to land with you. I know it was supposed to be me. But it's okay. They are your best friends."

I shook my head again. "NO!" I said, even louder that time. Everyone stopped to stare at me.

"It's okay," I said. "I don't need to get my legs." Rachel and Cora's mouths dropped open. "If my mom doesn't get to leave the ocean, I don't want to either."

"But Shyanna," Rachel said. "You've been so excited about going on land. It's all you've been talking about for weeks."

"Years, actually," Cora said.

I crossed my arms and shook my head. "No. I don't want to go to land without my mom."

Rachel started to cry. "But Shyanna! You and Cora are my best friends, and land and legs are half of who I am. Cora and I have been waiting for you to turn thirteen so we could visit Owen on land together."

My mom swam forward and put both hands on my cheeks. She leaned her forehead up against mine. "No, Shy," she said. "Your dad would want you to go on land. He loved having legs. He loved taking me to shore. I hoped I'd go with you, but I can't. I won't let you miss out on that part of your life for me."

"But mom . . ." I started to say.

"No. I insist, Shyanna. Please. Do it for me. Do it for your dad." She let me go and swam over and put one arm around Rachel and the other arm around Cora. "Do it for your best friends. But mostly, do it for you. It's what you've always wanted, and you deserve it."

They all were staring at me. Watching me. Waiting.

"Fine," I finally said. "But there's something I have to do first, before we go to land. There's someone I need to talk to."

"Well, you better do it fast," Cora said.

"Follow me," was my reply as I quickly swam out the door.

Chapter Nine

I swam toward the royal courtyard. Rachel, Cora, my mom, and Rachel's dad followed me without speaking. Cora's parents needed to stay home with the girls.

Even though it was almost midnight, Neptunia festivities were still going strong. We quickly swam to the entrance.

"Will you wait here?" I asked my mom. She frowned but nodded, and Rachel's dad said he would wait with her.

Rachel, Cora, and I swam to the royal guard. I whispered to him what I was there to do.

He nodded and swam ahead, leading us into the courtyard. Rachel and Cora each took one of my hands, and we swam together to the Queen. When she spotted us, she left her royal guests and swam over to greet us. She smiled when she reached us.

"Your baby sister is okay?" she asked Cora.

Cora nodded and squeezed my hand.

"What you did today was brave," the Queen said to me. "Swimming into the net to get Jewel out." She nodded at all three of us. "You mergirls are a constant surprise to the kingdom. Great singers, great spirit, and great bravery."

"Thank you," we all said. I bowed my head. Beside me, Rachel and Cora did the same thing.

"I've come to ask a favor," I told the Queen as humbly as I could.

The Queen nodded. "It's about your mom?" she guessed.

I nodded. "Yes."

I took a deep breath before I continued. "I know she wasn't supposed to expose herself to humans, but we all know she only did it to save me. She saved me and baby Jewel from being exposed and captured. If she hadn't done that, I wouldn't be here — neither would baby Jewel.

The Queen nodded again. "I know, Shyanna. You are very lucky."

"Her voice saved us," I said. "It was beautiful. It's such a shame she hasn't sung in so long. It wasn't easy for her to do it. She hasn't sung since my dad . . ."

I lowered my eyes to the sand on the bottom of the ocean floor. The Queen glanced at the King, who was sitting in his throne juggling sea sponges while a group of admirers cheered.

"I would like to hear her sing sometime. Maybe I could even sing with her." She turned back to me. "Don't you have somewhere you're supposed to be?" She glanced at my messed-up tail and my crazy hairdo. I saw her hide a smile. "Tonight is your leg ceremony, isn't it?"

"It's supposed to be," I told her.

She frowned ever so slightly.

"I was supposed to go to land with my mom," I told her. "I would still love to do that. She's all I have. I don't have a dad anymore, and I don't have any siblings. I only have my mom."

The Queen sighed.

"Is there any way you can use magic?" I asked. "Can you reverse her spell so she can use her legs again? She saved two lives! It was a selfless act. There must be exceptions. Can you please help me? Please?" I begged.

The Queen clicked her tongue, glanced at the King again, and then back to me.

"I wish I could help you," she said finally, "but I can't reverse the spell that quickly. No one can. It has to be done in stages. Other royalty will need to help — if they agree at all. It would have to go to vote,

which takes time," she added and then looked into my eyes. "You must go, Shyanna. Time is ticking. It's midnight or nothing to get your legs. That spell can never be reversed."

Rachel and Cora each grabbed one of my hands again. I needed the support.

"But my mom," I said.

"Go on," the Queen said. "Go. Get your legs. I will discuss this matter with the King. I can't promise you anything. But we will discuss it, you have my word."

"Thank you," I said with a bow.

The girls pulled me away, but I glanced over my shoulder at the Queen as we left the courtyard. She was already at the King's side. He caught my eye and winked. I'd done what I could. Now it was time to go.

"Come on!" Cora said. "It's getting late. We are running out of time!"

Outside the castle, the girls let go of my hands, and my mom took one. "Is everything okay?" she asked me.

"I hope so," I whispered.

On the way to shore, Mom asked me what I'd planned for the leg ceremony. I told her all about my spa day and the plans I had made with Star. When I was finished, she started to sing. Goosebumps ran along my arms, down my back, and all the way down my tail. Her voice was simply incredible. Rachel's dad swam to my other side, and he joined in and sang with her. It was perfect.

As the song ended, we got close to the shore. Mom let go of my hand. "Go," she said. "I can't go any farther. Your friends will go with you."

Rachel's dad stayed with her, but Cora and Rachel swam up with me. The moonlight lit up the shore. It was breathtaking. There was a path of white flowers leading up the beach. I glanced at the girls.

"All of us came to do it earlier as a surprise," Rachel said. "Right before Jewel got trapped."

"So that's why you were all out? That's when Jewel got in the net. It was all for me?" I asked.

"Did you think we'd forget your birthday?" Cora asked. "Don't be silly!"

"Come on, Shy. It's time," Rachel said, smiling.

I breathed in the night air, nervous and excited about what was about to happen. And then I opened my mouth and began to sing.

I saw Rachel and Cora grin. It was our song. The song we first sang together at the Melody Pageant. The song that would always represent our friendship.

Rachel and Cora swam slowly beside me, and then they stepped out of the water. I blinked, and they had their legs. Lovely long, graceful limbs.

They walked up to the beach on the flower path and turned, waiting for me. I moved slowly forward. My tail began to tingle. It got heavier and heavier, and then a weird sensation ran down my middle. It didn't hurt. It just felt odd.

A breeze hit my legs, and I looked down and realized my tail was gone. I wore a bathing suit bottom, the same color and texture as my tail. But instead of a fin, I had feet. I had toes. I even had knees. I lifted one leg, shook it out a little, and began to laugh.

"Walk!" Rachel shouted, and they both clapped and called out encouragement. I tried to take another step and fell flat on my face.

"Exactly what I did!" Cora hollered. "Try again."

I laughed and got up on my knees.

"Try again!" Cora screeched. "It gets easier!"

Rachel ran farther up the beach. "Come on, Shyanna!"

I got up from my knees, wobbling a little and then finding balance on my feet.

"Wow!" I said. And then I took a step and then another. "I'm doing it!" I cried. "I'm walking."

"Oh, yes you are!" Cora ran to my side.

"Have fun, girls!" a voice called out from under the ocean.

My mom. I couldn't see her, but I knew she was there. Watching and smiling.

"Be back before morning," she yelled.

"We will," I shouted into the night air. The oxygen filled my lungs in a different way than the ocean water did. It made me light-headed, and I giggled and threw out my arms and kicked my new legs.

"It's too late for Owen to be here," Rachel told me. "But we'll come back soon. The three of us."

The three of us skipped together in the dark night air, enjoying every minute. Before I knew it, the sun was rising. I glanced down at my legs, wiggled my toes, and then stepped back into the ocean. There would be more adventures on another day.

I only hoped my mom would be able to be a part of them.

Chapter Ten

"Hey, sleepyhead!" a voice called from outside my room.

I opened my eyes, and memories of the day before rushed into my head. It hadn't been exactly the birthday I'd planned, but it was still the best birthday I could imagine. There was drama, excitement, adventure, and a happy ending.

I stretched my arms over my head and remembered the feeling of having legs. I wiggled my tail around, happy to have it back but eager to try out my new legs another time. It was completely indescribable.

"We were all up late, but you must have worn yourself out having such a great time on land!" Mom said. "You slept past noon. It's time to get up!"

"It was so fun, though, especially skipping," I told her, but then my heart sank a little, knowing she might never be able to go on land again.

"Legs are so different from a tail," she said, swimming into my room and doing a somersault. "Breathing air always made me so giggly."

I nodded, watching her. She didn't look sad, but my heart still ached a little for her.

"Come on, Shyanna," she said. "I'll make fish-shaped pancakes for breakfast!"

"Okay!" I swam out of bed and flipped around the room to find a comfortable shell top to change into. Then I followed her to the kitchen.

"SURPRISE!" voices yelled when I swam into the kitchen.

I screamed in shock, and everyone started to laugh. Our kitchen was full of merboys and mergirls and their parents.

"Happy belated birthday!" everyone shouted. I glanced around, my hand still on my heart.

"Today you get the party you were supposed to have yesterday!" my mom said as she swam to me and gave me a giant hug.

Rachel and Cora swam close. "With pancakes and presents!" Cora shouted.

"And shrimp cake," Rachel added.

Everyone was chattering and smiling. It was amazing. I blushed at a loud version of "Happy Birthday," and my heart came close to bursting with happiness. Then someone shoved me into a decorated shell chair, and someone else started handing me presents to open.

"Oh my gosh," I said. "Birthday presents!"

"We know how much you love presents!" Cora said and laughed.

"And we heard you saved Cora's baby sister," Cassie said. "That's amazing, Shyanna. You deserve lots of presents."

I glanced over at my mom. She put her finger on her lips to signal for me not to say anything about her role in the rescue of Jewel. Across the noisy room, our eyes locked for a moment and I smiled at her, so thankful to have her for my mom.

"How were your legs?" asked a classmate who hadn't yet turned thirteen as she handed me another gift to open.

"Magical," I told her. "Simply magical."

Everyone kept talking and laughing as I opened present after present, feeling like the luckiest mermaid in Mermaid Kingdom. As I was stuffing my face with another piece of shrimp cake, a hush went over the room. It went from noisy to quiet in a second. I turned from the table to see the Queen of Neptunia looking at me. She carried a scroll of paper in her hand.

I glanced behind her, but she was alone. No King or guard.

"Hello, Shyanna. I'm looking for your mom," she said formally. No one else in the room uttered a sound. Everyone's eyes were on the Queen. It was pretty surreal.

"Yes?" my mom said, looking confused. The crowd around me parted, and Mom floated in beside me and tucked my hand in hers, as if offering me moral support. I glanced at her face, but she looked calm, not as terrified and jumpy as I felt.

"I come with news," the Queen announced. She turned to me. "Shyanna Angler has come to me and requested special use of Mermaid Magic to reverse the spell that has taken away your ability to use your legs on land."

Merpeople around the room gasped, and a low whisper buzzed as they gossiped about what had happened. The Queen lifted her hand, and it went silent again.

"Last night, the King and I called an emergency session with the Royal Council to discuss this interesting situation."

I held my breath.

She stared at my mom. "We've reached a decision."

No one said a word. I didn't even hear anyone take a breath. The Queen waited an extra moment for dramatic effect. She loved to perform, the Queen. She cleared her throat and opened the scroll and began reading from it.

"The Royal Council has decided to grant Emerald Angler use of her legs, even though she was seen by humans."

Everyone in the room gasped and started whispering.

The Queen held up her hand and waited for quiet.

"It is because of special circumstances. Two mermaid lives were saved, and thus we have decided to alter the magic for leg use. But there will be strict stipulations."

I squeezed my mom's hand tightly. My heart pounded so loudly I was sure everyone in the room could hear it.

"Emerald will be allowed to use legs on land, but only when accompanied by either mermaid she saved, Shyanna Angler or Jewel Bass."

The room erupted in chatter again.

"She saved Jewel?" some people asked. "What happened? What humans saw her?"

The Queen was finished, and she rolled up the scroll and swam forward, ignoring the chaos in the room. She swam to my mom and me, smiled, and handed over the scroll to my mom.

"What you did was very brave. I see where your daughter gets her bravery," the Queen said to my mom. She winked at me.

"I would like to hear you sing sometime," she said to my mom. "Perhaps a duet?"

My mom nodded quickly, and the Queen smiled and bowed her head.

"Thank you so much," I told her. I grinned. "Can I offer you and the King a slice of birthday cake? You can take it back to him."

"Salmon cake?" she asked.

"Shrimp," I told her.

"The King and I love a good shrimp cake," she said and patted my head.

I got her two large pieces and wrapped them up. When I finished, the Queen was laughing with my mom about something. I handed her the cake. "Thank you again," I said.

She accepted the cake. "The King is sorry he couldn't come along. He had a round of sea golf booked with another king and couldn't get out of it." She smiled brightly. "Try and stay out of trouble now, Shyanna," she said.

And then she was gone.

Mom put her mouth close to my ear. "After the party is over, you and I are going to land," she whispered.

"Are you sure?" I asked. It would be her first time on land since my dad disappeared.

"It's time," she said.

Rachel and Cora swam over to squeal with me. I looked at my mom. "Is it okay if my best friends come?"

She nodded. "I wouldn't want it any other way. These girls are like family!"

I told Rachel and Cora what we were going to do, and then we twirled in circles and did flips of excitement.

It was the best belated birthday party anyone had ever had. Even my biggest dreams couldn't compare. All of my wishes had come true.

Legend of Mermaids

These creatures of the sea have many secrets. Although people have believed in mermaids for centuries, nobody has ever proven their existence. People all over the world are attracted to the mysterious mermaids.

The earliest mermaid story dates back to around 1000 BC in an Assyrian legend. A goddess loved a human man but killed him accidentally. She fled to the water in shame. She tried to change into a fish, but the water would not let her hide her true nature. She lived the rest of her days as half-woman, half-fish.

Later, the ancient Greeks whispered tales of fishy women called sirens. These beautiful but deadly beings lured sailors to their graves. Many sailors feared or respected mermaids because of their association with doom.

Note: This text was taken from The Girl's Guide to Mermaids: Everything Alluring about These Mythical Beauties *by Sheri A. Johnson (Capstone Press, 2012). For more mermaid facts, be sure to check this book out!*

Talk It Out

1. Shyanna couldn't wait to turn thirteen and get her legs. What birthday are you looking forward to the most? Why?

2. Shyanna had a lot of drama on her birthday — from being alone to saving Jewel to her mom losing her land privileges, it was a crazy day. How do you think Shyanna handled herself during everything?

3. Do you think it was smart for Shyanna's mom to break the rules and distract the humans? What else could have been done?

4. Were you surprised that the Queen reversed the ruling about Shyanna's mom and her ability to go on land again? Why or why not?

Write It Down

1. If you could do anything in the world for your birthday, what would it be? Write a detailed plan about your dream birthday event.

2. Being a mermaid sounds fun, but it also seems dangerous. Using examples from the book, make a pro and con list about being a mermaid. According to your list, are you pro or con being a mermaid?

3. Write a newspaper article about the big rescue of baby Jewel.

4. Pretend you are Shyanna and write a journal entry about your birthday. Be sure to include how you were feeling during each event of the day.

About the Author

Janet Gurtler has written numerous well-received YA books. Mermaid Kingdom is her debut series for younger readers. She lives in Calgary, Alberta, near the Canadian Rockies, with her husband, son, and a chubby Chihuahua named Bruce. Gurtler does not live in an igloo or play hockey, but she does love maple syrup and says "eh" a lot.

About the Illustrator

Katie Wood fell in love with drawing
when she was very small. Since graduating
from Loughborough University School of
Art and Design in 2004, she has been living
her dream working as a freelance illustrator.
From her studio in Leicester, England, she
creates bright and lively illustrations for
books and magazines all over the world.

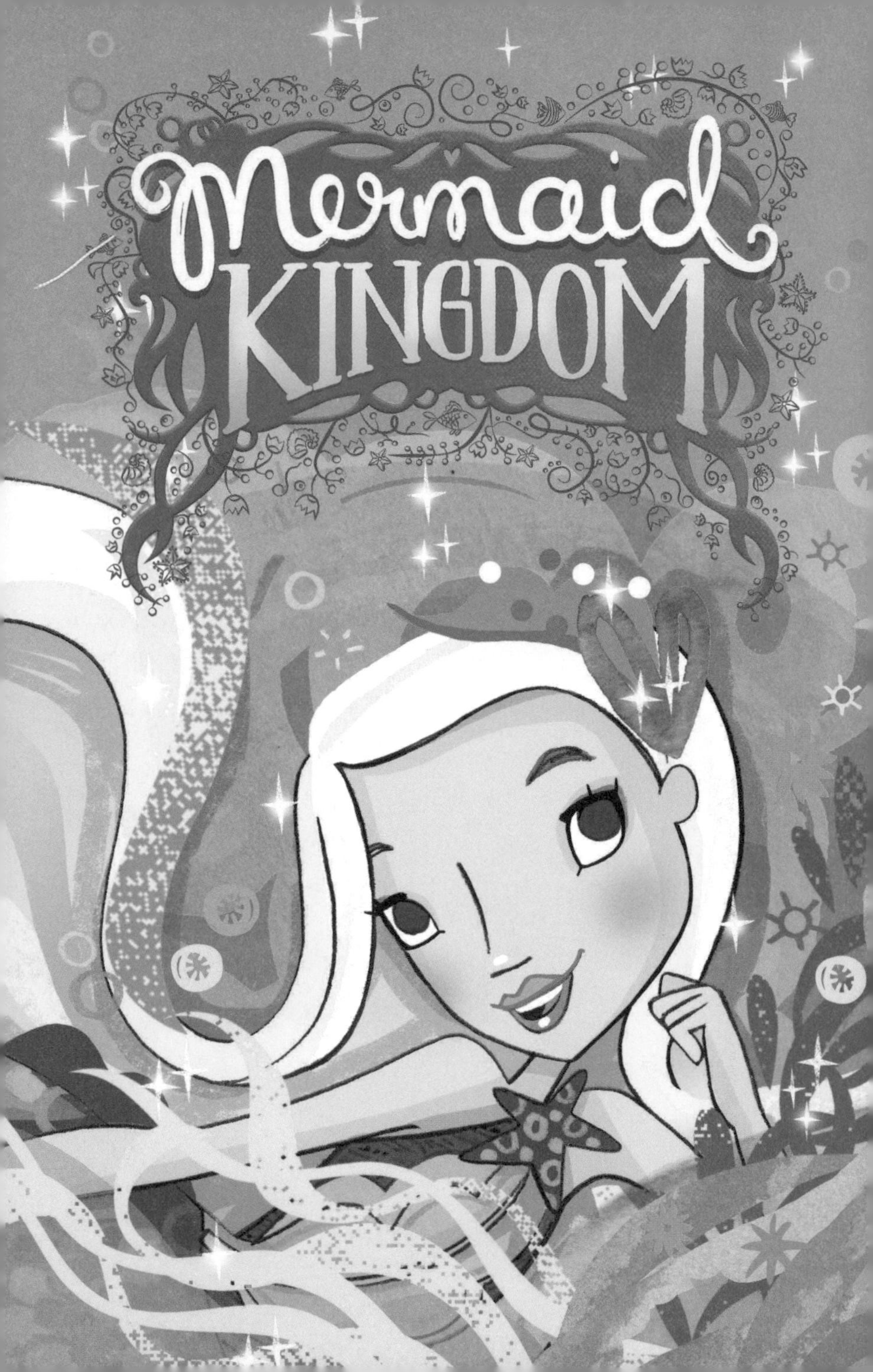
Mermaid
KINGDOM

Dive in and get swept away!

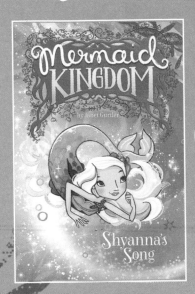

Mermaid KINGDOM
by Janet Gurtler

Shyanna's Song

Mermaid KINGDOM
by Janet Gurtler

Rachel's Secret

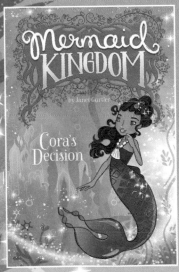

Mermaid KINGDOM
by Janet Gurtler

Cora's Decision

Mermaid KINGDOM
by Janet Gurtler

Shyanna's Wish